The Glo Friends live in a magical place called Glo Land. This colourful rhyming story tells of one of their adventures.

British Library Cataloguing in Publication Data

Woodman, June
    Glo Worm.—(Glo friends; 3)
    I. Title   II. Layfield, Kathie
    III. Series
    823'.914[J]   PZ7
    ISBN 0-7214-0974-1

First edition

Published by Ladybird Books Ltd Loughborough Leicestershire UK
Ladybird Books Inc Lewiston Maine 04240 USA

GLO Friends™

GLO Worm and the big freeze

written by JUNE WOODMAN
illustrated by KATHIE LAYFIELD

Ladybird Books

In such a lovely, secret place
Among the flowers and trees,
The cheerful Glo Friends live a life
Of happiness and ease.

Each Glo Friend has a tiny house
Well hidden, out of sight.
They call their country Glo Land for
It glows like stars at night.

They really are most charming folk,
And every day they try
To keep Glo Land a happy place,
Where no one needs to cry.

Young Glo Worm is the brightest one.
He has the best ideas.
He leads them on adventures and
Just laughs away their fears.

Glo Grannybug is old and wise.
She cooks them lovely food.
And young Glo Friends all cuddle up
They know she's sweet and good.

One night, Glo Grannybug calls them
To sit beside Glo Pond.
She tells a story from the past
Of which they're very fond.

"Now, pay attention," she calls out,
"And listen to me well,
For this is an important tale
That I'm about to tell.

Long years ago, the moon was full
As it will be tonight.
But then our Glo Friend family
Did not glow quite so bright.

Then suddenly, down through the dark,
There fell a magic spray
Of Moondrops – so we all set off
To get them, right away.

We brought them back and emptied them –
The pond filled to the top.
We all worked hard collecting them
And didn't spill one drop.

Now every time the moon is full,
We Glo Friends go and look
For Moondrops, falling from the sky
Into some secret nook.

These magic Moondrops help us to
Keep up our cheerful glow.
We always cover our Moon Pond
To keep it fresh you know."

"Go on, then," Baby Glo Worm says,
Excited as can be.
"Well, then those horrid Moligans
Came here to live, you see.

They'd dug a deep dark mine, where they
Expected to find gold.
Great torches lit their way, but it
Was smoky, wet and cold.

They thought, if they could catch a few
Bright Glo Friends, it would be
Much lighter down inside their mine –
Then gold they'd *surely* see."

"Oooh, they are horrid, wicked things!"
Glo Butterfly then said,
"I cannot listen any more,
I'm going home to bed."

"Don't worry," says Glo Grannybug.
"They're mean, but not so strong.
They'll NEVER harm our Glo Land for
Their plans always go wrong!"

Suddenly, some Moondrops fall.
They make a pattering sound.
"But that's no good," sad Glo Snail says.
"They're dripping underground."

"He's right, you know," Glo Worm agrees.
"The Moligans live there.
Still, it won't matter this time as
We've Moondrops left to spare."

So giggling and chattering,
Glo Friends go off to bed.
As they lay sleeping peacefully
The moon shone overhead.

Through every sunny summer's day
They're busy as can be.
They sip the Moondrops, smell the flowers,
And have friends round for tea.

But, even in this happy land
The skies aren't always clear;
Soon days grow dark, the nights grow cold,
And winter time is here.

The snowy flakes come floating down
All over hills and trees.
As it grows even colder, now
Glo Pond begins to *freeze*!

The Glo Friends wake when morning comes
And rub their sleepy eyes.
When they look through their windows they
Get *such* a big surprise.

Glo Worm worries when he sees
The pond all turned to ice.
The Glo Friends will get thirsty, and
That won't be very nice.

He runs to tell Glo Grannybug –
She's standing at her door.
"What we need now," she says, "is some
Quick way to make it thaw."

So Glo Worm tries to think, while all
His friends play in the snow.
Then suddenly a noise is heard –
Where *did* those Glo Friends go?

"The Moligans are coming here!"
The whisper goes around.
So quickly, in their hidey-holes
The Glo Friends go to ground.

Just see those noisy Moligans
Who stamp into the glade.
Their flaming torches spark and flare –
The Glo Friends are afraid.

Some rush into their houses, some
Are hiding in the snow.
But all of them find places where
They will be safe, they know.

Then they hear the leader shout,
"Some Glo Friends *must* be caught
To light our mine, and warm our hands;
To work they must be taught.

Just stick your torches in the snow,
Then prod and pry and poke!"
But they can't find a single one
Of those bright Glo Friend folk.

The cross and grumbling Moligans
At last go on their way.
But look! They have forgotten one
Big torch. Hip, hip hooray!

With shouts of joy the Glo Friends all
Come racing out to see,
Bright Glo Worm beaming proudly as
He holds a torch with glee!

With that hot flame, he melts the ice,
Although it is so thick.
Says gloomy Glo Snail, "I *do* wish
I'd thought of that – he's quick!"

Now Glo Worm scoops up sparkling drops
And pours them in a pot.
Each Glo Friend takes a little sip,
Quite soon they've drunk the lot!

They laugh and play so merrily,
Forgetting their bad fright.
Glo Grannybug makes pizzas, for
It's party-time tonight!